LION
ON THE
LOOSE

First published in 2008 in Great Britain by
Barrington Stoke Ltd
18 Walker Street, Edinburgh, EH3 7LP

www.barringtonstoke.co.uk

This edition first published 2022

Text © 2008 C.L. Tompsett
Illustrations © 2008 Alan Marks

A CIP catalogue record for this book is available
from the British Library upon request

ISBN: 978-1-80090-135-3

Printed in Great Britain by Charlesworth Press

LION ON THE LOOSE

C.L. TOMPSETT

Illustrated by
Alan Marks

Barrington Stoke

It was the school holidays and we had two weeks off. I wanted to go to the fair.

Mum said I could go if I took my little sister, Jess. "Jess likes the fair," Mum said.

I was a bit fed up. Jess was only 7. She liked the little rides. I liked the big ones.

At the fair there was a woman doing face painting.

"My name is Meg," the woman said to Jess. "Come and get your face painted. What would you like to be?"

"A lion," Jess said.

Meg looked at me. "This will take about 10 minutes," she said.

I left Jess with Meg and I went on the Big Dipper.

Then I went back to get Jess.

Wow! She looked just like a lion.

"The paint will stay on for a long time,"
Meg said.

On the way home from the fair, Jess
and I took a short-cut past the woods.

We saw some big paw prints in the wet mud near the trees.

"Let's follow them," I said.

We went into the woods and it began to get dark.

All of a sudden there was a loud roar.

Jess began to cry, so I held her hand.

I was afraid too.

We ran back out of the woods and went back home the long way.

At home Mum had the TV on. A news reporter was speaking. "There is a lion on the loose," he said.

I began to think about the paw prints.

I began to think about the roar.

"That lion is in the woods!" I yelled. "We saw the paw prints and we heard a roar."

Mum looked terrified.

"You must both stay in the house," she said. "It's not safe to go out till that lion is back behind bars."

At 7 p.m. Jess had a bath and went to bed.

She still looked like a lion.

The face paint had not washed off.

I went to bed at 10 p.m. and Mum went to bed a bit later.

I woke up in the middle of the night.

My cat, Tabby, was howling out in the garden.

I looked out of the window and saw Tabby. She had run up a tree.

Mum woke up too. "I'm going into the garden to see what's up," she said.

"I'll come with you, Mum," I said.

We both went out by the back door. We left it open.

There were big paw prints all round the tree.

Tabby was shaking. We called to her, but she didn't want to come down.

Mum phoned the police.

Two policemen came and looked in the garden.

"These are not cat prints," one of them said. "They are too big."

Tabby jumped down from the tree. She left tiny paw prints in the mud.

I picked Tabby up.

She was still shaking and she didn't want to go into the house.

"Let's see where these prints come from," one of the policemen said. "And let's see where they go to."

He followed the big prints.

I followed him.

And Mum followed me.

"That's very odd," he said as he followed the prints round the tree. "They seem to go back into the house."

I looked at them. He was right.

Mum and I were terrified. We ran back into the house. Tabby jumped out of my arms.

There were big muddy paw prints all over the carpet.

Some prints went up the stairs and some came down.

"Oh no!" Mum yelled. "Jess is in danger!"

Mum ran up the stairs.

The policeman ran after her.

"Stop there, madam," the policeman said. "It is not safe. I'll go."

The paw prints stopped at the door of Jess's room.

Mum let out a scream.

I was shaking with fear.

The policeman opened the door.

Jess was fast asleep.

There was no lion in there.

"I'm so glad you're safe," Mum said.
She held Jess tight.

One of the policemen said, "But that
looks like blood on her pillow."

"It's only paint," Mum said. "Jess had her face painted like a lion at the fair."

"Maybe she thought she was a lion too!" I said.

Jess smiled and let out a roar.

Our books are tested
for children and young people by
children and young people.

Thanks to everyone who consulted on
a manuscript for their time and effort in
helping us to make our books better
for our readers.